Printed in the United Kingdom. First printing, 2021

Illustrations by Coral Moon. Design by YOTE Design.com

The Cats of Dragon Hill

1

HE'S BACK

Sue Holland

For every child, everywhere.

CHAPTER 1

The panicked voice inside Gunner's head was getting louder and louder. 'Faster boy, faster!' With his ears pinned down by the strong northerly wind and his heart pounding in his chest, he could feel the road getting steeper. He emerged, exhausted, at the top of Dragon Hill.

Gunner could see his house in the distance, but would he make it that far? Who was this big cat chasing him? But time had run out. Gunner could feel the cat's long whiskers touching his tail.

CRUNCH.

Gunner yelped as he felt teeth sink deep into his skin. He sprinted down the garden path, shot through the cat flap, and skidded across the kitchen floor. Once in the lounge, he jumped up to the window seat and onto the safety of his favourite blanket. He looked warily out of the large bay window.

Staring straight back was *the* cat. He had matted grey fur and was *the* biggest and most fearsome cat that Gunner had ever seen. Gunner blinked, then swallowed hard as the cat narrowed his large and sinister amber eyes.

Who was he? And how could he possibly run that fast? Gunner was, after all, the fastest cat in the road. He looked at his tail; the beautiful stripes now ended abruptly in a painful stump. He gently licked the blood from around the wound; his tail was now an inch shorter.

Gunner had lived on Dragon Hill for just over two years, ever since he was a kitten. His beautiful pale ginger stripes and big wide eyes had made him irresistible to his owners. He was happy living in the road and had some good friends. There was little Puss who lived at the top of the hill, then Felix several doors away. Next-door-but-one to him was Sheba. He knew how lucky he was to have good and caring owners. Up until twenty minutes ago, he was very happy. His tail had stopped bleeding now. He looked up from his blanket; thankfully the mean cat had disappeared.

Gunner nervously poked his head through the cat flap for the fourth time that evening. It was Monday, and Monday was meeting night at the clubhouse. He was going to be late. This time he stepped through, one paw at a time, and tip-toed down the path. He darted towards the allotments, his eyes on full alert for the mean cat.

The clubhouse came into view. He had nearly made it! He couldn't wait to tell the others about the mean cat. What would they say?

The clubhouse was actually a large shed that had once been used by humans. It was now old and run-down and of no interest to them anymore. Gunner walked around the back and jumped in through the window.

Gunner put his nose in the air and breathed in the damp and musty smell. The big black hairy spider was still tucked in the corner of the dark ceiling. There were piles of sacking lying around, providing ample seating for all the cats. But Gunner headed straight towards the big old chair in the corner. The cream and gold one with a spring poking out from the back cushion.

'About time too,' said Sheba, grooming

herself whilst sitting neatly in the centre of the gold chair. 'I was beginning to think that you were going to be a no-show. I almost had to wait.'

Gunner sat on a sack instead. Sheba was a pure white Persian cat and very much a diva; she lived in the large house opposite Gunner. He watched her grooming her beautifully white soft fur. Her bright green eyes were bewitching.

A loud crash made both the cats jump as Felix stumbled in from the clubhouse kitchen. 'Sorry I'm late, got a bit distracted en route.'

'Huh,' snorted Sheba. 'What was it this time?'

Felix was your average-sized black and white moggy. His legs were mostly white, with big patches of black on his body and an all-black tail. His almond-shaped eyes stared across at Sheba.

'Er... well... you see, there was this cat flap and... such a lovely smell... succulent chicken pieces...'

'You mean you raided the neighbours again, Felix?' said Sheba. 'I'm not surprised you're looking a bit podgy. Have you thought about going on a diet?'

'I shall pretend I didn't hear that,' he replied, as he settled down next to Sheba's chair.

There was another disruption as Puss, the nervous little black cat from the top of the hill, made her way into the room and sat by the window.

'Well, as we are all here, shall we start the meeting?' said Felix.

'Oh, my goodness Gunner! What on

earth has happened to your beautiful tail?' gasped Puss.

Sheba and Felix stared down at the sorry sight.

'Well, if you don't have any objections, I will start the meeting,' said Gunner. 'It appears that we have been joined in the neighbourhood by a rather unsavoury character, and he is a force to be reckoned with. As you can clearly see, I am no longer the fastest cat on Dragon Hill.' Gunner looked down at his tail. He explained to Sheba, Felix and Puss that he had been minding his own business at the bottom of the hill when out of nowhere, he was chased by a huge, mean and scary cat. 'How could a fat cat be that quick, and so mean?' he asked the others.

'Tell me more about him Gunner. Did

he have any other distinguishing features?' asked Sheba, looking unusually interested.

'Yes, he had a large piece missing out of his right ear and one of his fangs had been broken in half.'

'Oh no! It can't be!' said Sheba.

'What Sheba? Spit it out,' wailed Gunner.

'There used to be a mean cat who lived in the bungalow at the bottom of the road many years ago. He terrorised the neighbourhood!'

'Oh no,' shivered Felix. 'IT'S HIM, IT'S ROSCO, HE'S BACK!'

CHAPTER 2

'So, what are we going to do? If it is this Rosco, we're all in danger. He definitely wants to be king of the hill and he's taking no prisoners,' said Gunner.

'I don't think I want to walk back on my own,' said Puss, looking anxiously out of the window.

'We need a plan to get rid of him, once and for all,' said Felix firmly.

'What are you thinking Felix?' asked Sheba. 'Tell us.'

'You're not going to like it, Sheebs. Not one little bit.'

'Don't call me Sheebs, Felix, you make me sound so common. My name is Sheba, named after the Queen of Sheba. Make sure you use it in future.'

'This is no time to be a diva, Sheba. Now listen up. We're gonna need help and we're gonna need a plan. WE NEED VINNIE!' demanded Felix, banging his paw down on the table.

'No, no, no, definitely not! Not Vinnie. I just couldn't bear it,' said Sheba.

'Who is this Vinnie?' asked Gunner, pricking up his ears.

'Vinnie is Rosco's cousin. They both came down together from London many years ago, but they fell out.'

'But Felix... do we have to ask Vinnie for help? He's so... you know, vile.'

'Yes, Sheba, we do. Vinnie is excellent at making a plan and this is his old stomping ground, and besides, I'm sure he'd jump at the chance to get Rosco back for what he did.'

'How do we find this Vinnie?' asked Puss.

'I know where to find him,' said Felix.

The cats all agreed that they would set off home together, now that the meeting had come to a close. Felix was placed in charge of contacting Vinnie.

Vinnie had once lived at the bottom of Dragon Hill but now lived in the next street, Church Street. In the daytime, especially if it was chilly outside, he could be found in the warmth of the hairdressing salon, moving from cosy lap to cosy lap, being stroked and pampered by many kind and friendly customers. But in the summer, when the weather was too warm, he would saunter into the church where the hard-stone floor was wonderfully cool against his thick brown tabby mane of fur. In the evenings, especially if he was in a particularly mischievous mood, he would climb over the fence into the tree nursery, sharpen his claws on the many young trees and then wee against the new shiny tractor whenever he felt the need. Vinnie didn't want to be owned by anyone. He wanted to be free; free to come and go wherever and whenever he pleased.

Gunner couldn't see Rosco from his window. He decided to make a dash for it over to Sheba's house; it was only on the opposite side of the road. Not far at all. He walked stealthily down the path, then shot across the road, leapt over the gate, down her path, up onto the wheelie bin, then leapt high onto the shed.

Oh no! He could see Rosco staring at him with those scary amber eyes from the middle of Sheba's back garden. Gunner froze. Now what? He thought for a moment, then leapt onto the trampoline where he was propelled high up into the sky, landing conveniently on Sheba's veranda.

'Quick Gunner, inside,' said Sheba beckoning him in. Felix and Puss were already there so Sheba quickly closed the glass door.

'That was some entrance Gunner, very impressive,' said Felix.

'Oh, my goodness Gunner, you were so brave; you must have been scared. I wish I had your courage,' stammered Puss. The cats all stared out through the window at Rosco from the safety of Sheba's lounge.

Felix had met up with Vinnie and a meeting had been arranged for Friday evening at seven pm.

'You mustn't be late anyone; I don't like it when cats or humans are late.'

'Don't worry, Sheba, we'll be bang on time. We'll see you at the hidey hole at seven on the dot.'

Sheba rolled her eyes, 'It's not the hidey hole, Felix, it's the clubhouse,' she tutted.

CHAPTER 3

At 6.45 on Friday evening, Felix, Puss and Gunner waited for Sheba on her veranda. They would all be going to the clubhouse together – safety in numbers.

'It's so spooky walking through the allotments at night,' whispered Sheba.

'Stick close to me Sheebs, I'll look after you. Don't worry,' croaked Felix.

'But I am worried, Felix. It's all right for you, you've got some black camouflage; my white fur lights up like a beacon. I'll be seen for miles and Rosco's bound to spot me.'

'WHOA! what's that?' squealed Puss, spotting a tall figure staring right at her.

'It's only a scarecrow, Puss, it's not a real human,' sighed Gunner, his heart beating fast. As the clubhouse came into sight, they could see movement from inside.

'He's here! Vinnie's already here!' whispered Felix.

Gunner was the first to leap in through the window. He waited in the kitchen as the other cats followed one by one.

'You go in first Sheba, Vinnie knows you,' said Gunner, pushing her forward. As she walked into the room, Sheba stopped and stared; it had been a long time since she and Vinnie had last set eyes on each other. Sat perched up high on the long table, with his large paws crossed over one another, he resembled a king looking down on his people. He still had presence but his once glossy brown striped fur was now looking a bit dull and lifeless, and he was definitely heavier. His eyes, large and green with a hint of amber, narrowed as he grinned. He had quite a few pieces missing from his ears from the many fights he'd been in.

'Allo Darling, 'he smirked.

'Good evening, Vincent,' Sheba replied, walking over to a low stool furthest away, jumping up then starting to groom her paw.

Felix entered the room next and gave a nervous half smile to Vinnie.

'Allo me old china plate, how's it going?' said Vinnie.

'Why did he call Felix a china plate, Gunner?' whispered Puss in the kitchen.

'Vinnie's a Londoner. I think it's rhyming slang for mate,' he whispered back.

Gunner and Puss walked in nervously together.

'And oo do we ave ere then, a couple of wise guys?' teased Vinnie, pulling on one of his whiskers.

'Girl actually,' mumbled Puss.

Sheba stood up. 'This is Gunner and this is Puss,' she announced as they walked past. Vinnie looked at Gunner's shortened tail with its crusty scab.

'Now, listen up everyone,' said Felix. 'Vinnie is here to help us, aren't you Vinnie? You're going to help us with a plan to get rid of Rosco.'

'I sure am, and the pleasure will be all mine. But it's not going to be just any old plan, this needs to be special and well-thought-out. But first, get me a saucer of beer, Sheba, there's a good gal.'

CHAPTER 4

Sitting in the morning sunshine, Puss sighed happily and stretched out on her front doorstep. She loved the weekends; her owners didn't have to rush off early in the morning, meaning plenty of time for strokes and cuddles. She was even allowed to sit on top of the ironing basket and could get away with sleeping on the new cream rug. She lived at the top of the hill across the road from the tall cherry tree. Puss liked to sit halfway up the tree on her favourite branch. It was too scary going higher than that. But from her branch she could watch everything that was going on in the road. Only now, Rosco had discovered that this was a good viewing place too. This was going to be his tree from now on, and sharing was not an option.

As the sun beat down onto her soft black fur, Puss yawned. It was time for a nap. But who was that walking up the hill? Wait a minute, she thought, that's Vinnie and Gunner.

Seeing the two cats march up the hill together gave Puss a warm feeling of protection. She hadn't ventured far since the arrival of Rosco. As they strode up towards the house, she ran out to greet them. 'Hey guys, have you seen him? Is he around today?'

'Yep, we've spotted him alright,' said Vinnie, inspecting the cherry tree with Gunner. 'I knew the paunchy dirtbag would be there this morning.'

'And where's that?' asked Puss.

'Why, down in the field, terrorising the

wildlife of course,' said Vinnie.

'Should have seen the blighter, Puss. You wouldn't Adam and Eve it, he snatched a mouse with his paw, tossed it up high in the air and caught it in his jaws as it came down, CRUNCH.'

Puss gasped.

'Bit his head off in one large bite!' shuddered Gunner. 'Just like my tail.'

'Golly' said Puss. I've never caught a mouse. Have you?'

'I don't bother any more Puss, don't have the need. My owners give me such a tasty variety of food. Chicken, fish, snacks on offer throughout the day and even roast beef on a Sunday.'

'Sheba says catching mice is so yesterday,' said Puss

'Makes a mess on her soft white fur too,

no doubt,' added Vinnie.

Vinnie, Gunner and Puss continued to patrol up and down Dragon Hill, thoughtfully piecing together their new plan - operation Rosco.

Later that day, Gunner looked out of the window and saw movement in the hedge. Staring hard and trying to make out what it was, he glimpsed a pair of scary amber eyes.

'Oh no! He's there waiting to pounce on me, how can I get to the clubhouse now?'

Just at that moment, Gunner's owners were getting ready to leave the house to go over to Sheba's place. Gunner stayed close by, weaving in and out between their legs as they started to walk down the path.

'Ahh, look Michael,' said Gunner's owner. 'Gunner wants to come to supper with the Johnsons too; he's following us.'

'Cor, that was a close one tonight,' puffed Gunner, arriving at Sheba's veranda.

'Come on everyone, stay close, let's get to the hangout,' urged Felix.

'Oh, for goodness sake Felix, it is not the hangout, it's the clubhouse!' shrieked Sheba.

Vinnie was already sitting calmly on the table, having drunk his beer from the saucer. The cats walked in one by one.

'Evening ruffians, do take a pew,' said Vinnie, letting out a large and smelly belch.

'Oh, for goodness sake, Vinnie, you really haven't changed a bit, have you? You're so vulgar,' muttered Sheba, picking up her nail file.

'Why change perfection, darling?'

'Now, let's get on with the job at hand, shall we everyone?' said Felix.

'Right,' said Vinnie, clearing his throat.

27

He then started coughing, it seemed to go on for ages.

'Is he alright?' asked Puss. After one last huge unexplained and horrible noise, Vinnie coughed up a large furball. It landed on the floor next to Sheba.

'Yuck, that's gross Vinnie, and just remember, you're a guest here in our clubhouse,' reminded Sheba.

'A guest who's become a pest,' whispered Felix.

'Right, where was I?' Vinnie explained to the cats that they would be taking turns to spy on Rosco. 'We have to have an exact timetable of where and when he goes for the plan to work. I've drawn out a detailed chart of who's doing what. Gunner, you're on first shift tomorrow morning. On Wednesday evening we'll meet back here and... erm...

what's that word?'

'Confer, Vinnie, it's confer.'

'Thank you, darling, yes confer all our findings. Then we can begin to put our plan into action, and some action it's gonna be. Now be a sweetie and go and get me a snack, I'm Hank Marvin.'

Puss looked over at Gunner. 'Hank Marvin? What does he mean?'

'Starving, Puss. He's starving,' replied Gunner.

CHAPTER 5

Gunner stepped out of his cat flap at two in the morning under a brilliant white crescent moon. Everything looked so different. There was very little cloud tonight, and the sky wasn't as dark as he would have liked. He had to be vigilant. His was the first shift and his heart was now thumping in his chest.

Creeping up the hill and looking from side to side, Gunner stopped and crouched under a parked car. The scary amber eyes were nowhere to be seen. It was safe to continue. Now at the top of the hill, he hurried past Puss's house then bolted down the slope. He hid under another parked car. It seemed almost too silent, but then Gunner wasn't used to being out at this time, perhaps it was like this every night. How he wished he was snuggled up in a small ball on his cosy green blanket. Must keep going, he thought, no time for anything else.

Tiptoeing silently into the garden opposite the empty bungalow, Gunner started to crawl into the coal bunker. The entrance was tight; Vinnie could never have squeezed in. He wriggled and wriggled and, at last, he was through! He made himself as comfortable as he could. Now, all he had to do was to watch and wait... and try not to fall asleep!

If anything, it was boring on night-watch duty. Dragon Hill was still and quiet, with nothing much moving until a noisy Tawney owl hooted in the oak tree above. How miserable it must have been for the cats when Rosco had lived here before. Why had he left? And more importantly; why had he returned?

As dawn started to break, Gunner's ears pricked up as he heard a familiar noise: the bang of a cat flap. There he was! Rosco was on the driveway of the empty bungalow. Yawning, then stretching out his big framed body, Rosco trotted towards the field. But something made him stop. He looked up towards the tree. The tawny owl hooted, flapped his large wings then flew off. Gunner swallowed and his tail started to twitch. Please don't look into the coal bunker.

After waiting for some time, Gunner thought it would be safe to leave his hiding place; Rosco had been gone for a while. Squeezing his cold and stiff body through the small opening, he dragged himself home stopping off at Puss's house to report his findings.

Safely back home, Gunner gobbled up his breakfast then jumped onto his blanket to start cleaning the soot from his fur.

'Where have you been?' asked his owner. 'You're filthy, absolutely black!'

Puss breathed in heavily, it was her turn to be on watch. She took the first step towards the field.

'You can do this Puss, all you have to do is watch Rosco from afar, it's perfectly safe, he won't even see you,' she muttered to herself.

She took another few steps. Her legs were trembling. What if he saw her? She was almost at the edge of the field now. There was nowhere to hide. What if he ran at her?

'I can't! I just can't do it,' she cried, turning quickly and running back home as fast as her little legs would carry her.

CHAPTER 6

Vinnie was first to arrive at the clubhouse that evening. He took his place on the table. The plan was starting to take shape. With help from the cats on Dragon Hill, it was going to work.

Vinnie waited for the other cats to arrive. Rosco hadn't always been his enemy. Not in the old days. They had been best buddies at one time, back in London, in the upstairs flat above the pub. They were always getting into scrapes and jams of course, but they were mates, and they always stuck together. Then they had wound up in Dragon Hill.

It was one cold wintery Saturday morning and Rosco and Vinnie were strolling along the high street.

'Cor, look at those chicken legs, Vin. I'm

as hungry as an alligator in a swamp,' said Rosco, licking his lips and staring through the big glass window of the butcher's shop. They came up with a plan to distract the butcher and steal a chicken leg or two. Only... the plan went wrong!

They weren't expecting the butcher's wife to suddenly appear in the shop. She chased them out with a broom, and Rosco, being the fastest, escaped first. He always waited and held the door or window open for Vinnie to follow, but not this time. He shut the door in Vinnie's face leaving Vinnie trapped! Rosco didn't help his friend, instead, he scampered off, his mouth clamped down firmly onto a chicken leg. The butcher gave Vinnie a good slap and he was thrown out of the shop. His bruised back ached for weeks. Rosco was nowhere to be seen when Vinnie returned home to the bungalow. So, yes, it was now pay back time: Rosco was going to get what was coming to him.

Gunner, Felix and Sheba arrived on time, with Sheba bagging the gold chair, as usual.

'Where's the beer then?' asked Vinnie, staring down at Sheba.

'Fetch it yourself, I'm not your servant', she snapped back, breathing in hard and pointing her nose high into the air. Puss entered the room and edged her way over to the seat by the window, head hung low.

'Good evening Puss', scowled Sheba.

'Or should that be Wuss?' snapped Felix.

'So, Puss, owners couldn't be bovered to give you a proper name, eh?'

'Something like that, Vinnie', she sighed unhappily.

'You let us all down, Puss!' snarled Felix.

'I'm surprised you had the nerve to show your face tonight.'

'I'm sorry, I was scared.'

'And you think we weren't?' asked Felix

'Well, let's get on with things, shall we?' said Gunner.

Sheba started sniffing the air, then pulled a face. 'Did you just make that horrible smell Vinnie?'

Vinnie smirked. 'Oh, shut it diva, you're not so wonderful yourself. I've seen you washing your bottom on the veranda.'

'Now now children, put your claws away,' said Felix.

Sheba glared at Felix. 'Huh! You're supposed to be on my side, you adore me, remember?' It was of course true; Felix did adore Sheba even though she was a diva. But it wasn't her fault; her owners spoilt her

37

rotten. They gave her the very best of food and the latest top-of-the-range bedding. Her scratching post station was something to be seen; in fact, Felix was most envious of it. He would never get tired or bored with that in his lounge. What with all the posts, balls and toys swinging invitingly down. Felix didn't have a scratching post but he was happy sharpening his claws on the front arm of the sofa. There was nothing more pleasing than a good old scratch. He didn't understand though why his owners went red in the face and started shouting. He decided they must be playing a game so he continued to claw and tear at the sofa. He was most pleased with his efforts when he broke through the fabric to the foam one day. Small pieces of white stuffing fell out and floated through the air. It was such fun and looked so pretty it reminded him of when it snowed one year.

'Felix, are you listening?' asked Gunner.

'Sorry Gunner, I was miles away.'

Vinnie cleared his throat. 'Now everyone, this is what's gonna happen. Rosco always walks up Dragon Hill on Thursdays, just before noon, according to Felix's report. He then stops at the bush and teases some poor unsuspecting mouse before gobbling him up for lunch.'

'It's horrible! You wouldn't believe what he does. I saw it with my own eyes,' shivered Felix.

'Puss,' continued Vinnie. 'You'll be hiding in the cherry tree. When Rosco spots you, leap down and start running towards the bottom of the hill.'

Puss looked up at Vinnie, most alarmed. 'But.... but, you're using me as bait!' she wailed.

Vinnie pointed his paw towards Gunner. 'Gunner, you'll be at Felix's house. When you see Puss running towards you with Rosco hot on her tail, you intercept and Puss will then run into Sheba's house. Rosco will now be chasing you Gunner. It's most important that you keep a distance from the blighter but you're the fastest, and by this point you won't have far left to go.'

Gunner gulped with fear. He'd had Rosco on his tail before, quite literally.

'Are you listening Gunner,' snapped Vinnie. Gunner nodded. 'When you reach your house, you must speed up, it's vital to get over the netting as quickly as possible I'll be up in the tree with Sheba and Felix The second you're off the netting, we'll pul it up as quick as a flash, hopefully with Rosco trapped safely inside. We'll have the blighter then.' Vinnie looked down at everyone, rubbing his paws together in excitement. 'So, what do you think of the plan everyone?'

'I think it's going to work, Vinnie!' blurted out Felix. 'I really do believe it's going to work.'

'It better had; I want that toe rag gone!' spat Vinnie. 'He left me for brown bread.'

'Brown bread?' said Puss puzzled.

'DEAD, Puss, he left me for dead! Don't you know nothing?' snorted Vinnie.

Sheba jumped up. 'Take me home, Felix, we're done here for tonight.'

'Back here tomorrow night. Everyone in the shed, and make sure you do what's on the list I've given you. IS THAT CLEAR? I can get quite angry if people don't pull their weight, and you don't want to see me angry.'

Sheba tutted.

'What's that for?'

'It's not the shed, Vinnie, it's the clubhouse, how many times do I have to repeat myself?'

CHAPTER 7

Sheba was first to arrive at the allotments the next morning. Leaping up onto the bench she started to groom herself. Vinnie was next to arrive.

'I'm going up into the tree. I'll take first watch so make sure you get the netting done today,' he demanded as he jumped up onto the first branch. Sheba's ears pricked up, there was someone coming. She gasped and looked up at Vinnie. 'Don't worry, it's just Puss, carry on.'

Puss appeared in the clearing; she was muttering to herself.

'I could hear you talking Puss,' said Sheba. 'Who you were talking to? I can't see anyone.'

'It's just Tiger, he's my friend. He's

43

standing next to me, but you won't be able to see him,' she said, jumping up onto the bench.

'I feel so much safer when Vinnie's here, don't you Sheba?' asked Puss staring up at Vinnie in the tree.

'As much as I don't like him, I have to agree. Come and help me with the camouflage netting.'

Vinnie looked down at the two cats. 'Ah, Puss, I hear you've brought your imaginary friend with you today,' he teased.

'He's not imaginary Vinnie, it's just that you can't see him. Tiger is sitting on the bench now and looking straight up at you.'

There was a rustle in the long grass as Gunner came running over. He came to a sudden halt; his back leg rose up onto his stretched-out neck as he started scratching vigorously. 'Ahh, that's better, that feels sooo good,' he sighed, giving the other side of his neck a good hard scratch too.

'Don't get too near to Gunner, Puss, he's got fleas,' blurted out Sheba.

'Don't be such a snob, Sheba. We all have fleas, only some of us don't care to admit it,' remarked Gunner.

'Well, I don't,' insisted Sheba. 'My owners give me flea drops every month without fail.' Gunner thought back to earlier that morning. His owners were scratching themselves too. Sheba was probably right.

'You need the drops, Gunner,' piped up Puss. 'Tiger says you need the drops too.'

'Who the heck is Tiger? I'm not having those drops on my beautiful fur, they burn my skin and besides, they've got to catch me first. I'm far quicker than them,' boasted

Gunner.

Gunner, Puss and Sheba set to work on camouflaging the netting. They used leaves mud and twigs.

'That looks pretty good guys, even if I do say so myself,' said Gunner looking at their hard work. 'It does look like that muddy patch covered in leaves at the bottom o the hill. But where's Felix today? It's not like him to be late, I hope Rosco hasn't got him pinned down somewhere.'

'He's fine, Gunner.'

'Who said that?'

'Up ere,' called out Vinnie, balancing uncomfortably on a high branch to get a better view.

'Good spot, Vinnie.'

'Don't worry about me old china plate I've just spotted the old boy, he's fine, he's just coming out of the Doctor's house in a bit of a panic.'

'The Doctor's!' cried Sheba, looking alarmed. 'But they've just got two new dogs! Felix doesn't like dogs.'

As Felix had been running late, he thought he would take a short cut through the Doctor's garden. As he approached the cat flap, he stopped, mesmerized by it. Delicious smells were drifting through the air, how could he resist? Just a little peek to see if there was anything on offer. He put his head inside the kitchen; steam was rising from the freshly prepared bowl of warm sausages cut up neatly into bite size pieces. One of his favourites, mmm. No noise, no movement: the coast seemed to be clear. He crept silently in. As Felix got nearer, he started to lick his lips. But what was that other smell?

'OH NO! DOGS!'

He hated dogs. Two huge black and brown ones came bounding into the kitchen. As Felix turned and made a run for it, his claws skidded on the slippery new kitchen floor. He thought he was done for but the dogs were skidding everywhere too. He hurtled through the cat flap and scampered off towards the allotments.

'Felix! Where have you been? you're late!' hissed Sheba, wagging her tail.

'I... erm...'

''You've been in the doctor's house, haven't you? Tell the truth now.' All the cats were now staring at Felix.

'Well... you see, Sheba,' he said panting.

'Why is your fur standing up on end? Well? we're waiting?' insisted Sheba, frowning and tapping her claws impatiently on the bench. Felix looked up and saw Vinnie glaring at him from up in the tree. Felix knew he'd been rumbled.

'I didn't steal anything, honest. I was just interested to see what was on offer,' he pleaded.

'Eh up, what's going on over there then?' called out Vinnie, staring across at the field.

'What's going on Vin? What can you see from up there?' asked Gunner.

'I've got Rosco in my view and he's just started on lunch. I won't share the gory details, except to say that there is one less blackbird on this earth.'

Puss shuddered.

'And his lunch isn't over yet, he just about to start on dessert,' called out Vinnie, still transfixed.

'Another blackbird?' asked Felix.

'Let's just call it Tira-mouse-su.'

'Oh no, that's horrid,' said Gunner. Vinnie climbed down from the tree.

'Let's get back while the blighter is busy with his meal. Gunner, help me hide the netting. And Sheba, I'll see you later tonight, darling. Back at the Love Shack,' he teased.

'Oh, for goodness sake, Vinnie, you're gross, and it isn't the love shack, as you so crudely put it, it's THE CLUBHOUSE,' she bellowed.

CHAPTER 8

Puss stood up, licked herself then sat back down again. She couldn't settle. Her afternoon nap was normally most enjoyable, dozing in the afternoon sunshine without a care in the world and dreaming of weekends, strokes and cuddles. She trotted upstairs and jumped up onto the landing windowsill. Her eyes grew wide with fear.

Rosco was striding up the hill. Puss gulped as he stopped and stared right at her, tightening his scary amber eyes. What would happen when she came face to face with him tomorrow? Would she freeze with nerves on seeing that big angry face glaring right at her? She couldn't let the cats down again; she had to find the courage from somewhere. Or tell Vinnie tonight that she couldn't go through with it. She didn't know which would be worse.

All the cats were muttering in the kitchen at the clubhouse on Wednesday evening.

'I don't understand it? He's normally here by now,' cried Sheba, sauntering into the room and taking the best chair.

Felix followed close behind. 'I think it's time you let me sit there, Sheebs. The floor is very hard for my poor old bottom.'

'What part of princess don't you understand, Felix?' she replied.

'Well, if you were a true princess, you would be kind and gracious and offer me your seat.'

'Well, it's not going to happen.'

'You can go off cats you know Sheba?' said Felix, trotting over to the other side of the room and plonking himself next to Puss.

'Well, at least I am not named after a common cat food,' she smirked.

'Well, actually Sheba...' grinned Gunner.

There was a thud in the kitchen; everyone looked up at the door.

'He's here!' whispered Felix. Standing in the doorway was Vinnie, except that it didn't look like Vinnie. All the cats gasped. His once bedraggled and lacklustre fur had been groomed and trimmed. His teeth had been cleaned and a smart new collar was sitting neatly around his neck. All the cats watched as Vinnie jumped up onto the table and took his usual place.

'Wow Vin!' blurted out Felix. 'You scrub up pretty good, that's really most impressive.'

Vinnie didn't say anything, he just grinned.

'Cor, Vin, you've even had your claws

53

clipped into shape, they must have had to get out the big guns for that, the chainsaw!'

Gunner leant over to Sheba and whispered, 'You can put a dog in a stable but you can't make it a horse.' Sheba sniggered.

'You may well scoff, but I have friends in high places, you know.'

'Who's that then Vin, old Tawny owl in the big oak tree?' sniggered Felix.

'Actually, you may well have heard of him, he's a second cousin of mine, is old Lazzer.'

There was a look of puzzlement on the cats' faces.

'Mm, Lazzer. No, it doesn't ring any bells,' said Sheba, looking thoughtful.

'Well, you'd probably know him as Larry. Larry from 10 Downing Street.'

The cats let out a gasp.

'Are you serious, Vinnie?'

'We used to hang out together when I lived in the old smoke, taught him everything he knows,' stated Vinnie, looking down at his neatly trimmed claws.

'So, you're related to Larry, the prime minister's cat?' gasped Gunner, looking most shocked. He didn't know if Vinnie was being serious.

'Did you get to go inside No. 10? And did you meet the big man?'

'I may have done, Felix, once or twice.'

'I can't quite believe it, Vinnie,' said Sheba, staring at him with her azure eyes wide open.

'Now, listen up everyone, we're gonna go over and over that plan till we know it off by heart, upside down, back to front, and inside out. Is that clear?' commanded Vinnie.

Sheba was now studying the side profile of Vinnie's face. He did actually resemble Larry from No.10, she thought. There was a definite likeness.

Gunner stood up to speak. 'Before we do Vinnie, I have a question for you.'

'You may speak.'

'Why did Rosco leave, and why has he now chosen to return?'

'I will tell you. Years ago, Vinnie and I came down from London. We stole a ride in a removals van. It pulled up on Dragon Hill, near the bungalow at the bottom. The owner of the bungalow, Mrs Gotobed saw us looking lost and hungry and took us in. All was well until Rosco let me down badly one day in the butcher's shop on the High Street. I went back home to have it out with him but the scallywag had gone, moved on.'

Vinnie's tail thumped up and down angrily.

'But how did you end up on Church Street, Vin?' asked Felix.

'Well, Mrs Gotobed moved out of the bungalow, she moved up to London to live with her daughter and grandchildren. I didn't fancy moving back to the smoke so I walked out through the cat flap and didn't return. I wandered around for a few hours and ended up in Church Street where I saw the hairdressing salon. Humans were chatting, and laughing, it looked so inviting so I poked my head around the door. They made such a fuss of me; I would have been a right idiot if I passed that one by. Loved me they did, still do.'

'But didn't Mrs Gotobed try to find you?'

'No, she knew I wasn't particularly fond of children. I got a right telling off once for scratching and biting one of the littl‹ blighters. They had it coming to ther though, they kept poking me with a crayo and tugging on my tail.'

'Oh,' piped up Puss. 'A missing cat wh‹ wasn't missed at all, that's sad.'

Vinnie continued. 'Anyway, Rosc obviously hasn't found it easy living on th street and probably made a few enemie‹ so he's returned here. He clearly wants to b the king of the hill, plus the bungalow is sti empty until the new humans move in.' Vinni stared down at Puss. 'What's up Puss? I ca tell you want to say something, spit it out.'

'I... I... don't like heights very much, an Tiger says it's best that I don't go up in th tree tomorrow.'

'Well, that's just too bad, there isn anyone else, and it's too late to change th plan. Now go and sit down,' he growled. 'Are there any more annoying cats with even more annoying questions or can we AT LAST PROCEED?!' belted out Vinnie at full volume.

After two hours of finely tuning operation Rosco, Sheba stretched out her paws and yawned. 'Come on Vinnie, we're all exhausted now.'

'Yes, let's bring this meeting to an end. We all know what we have to do tomorrow, don't we?' said Gunner, squinting his eyes and glaring at Puss.

'Okay, okay, I hear what you're saying. Let's go and get some shut eye, some of you need your beauty sleep. Ere darling, take my saucer out into the kitchen with you, there's a good gal,' said Vinnie. The clubhouse shook as Vinnie did one of his loud and smelly belches.

'You're just so vulgar Vinnie, I thought you had changed when I saw you tonight,' sighed Sheba.

'What does vulgar mean?' asked Puss.

'It means uncouth, no manners,' replied Felix.

'What does uncouth mean?'

'Look it up in the dictionary, Puss.'

'I was only asking.'

Vinnie stared over at Sheba who was now filing her claws yet again.

'And tell me this babe, what do you have that is so amazing? As far as I can see from where I'm sitting, there is just a diva who only loves one person... herself.'

'What I have, Vinnie, is refinement and sophistication,' said Sheba, tossing her head high up into the air. 'Something you will never have.'

Vinnie responded by letting off wind. It started as a small squeak, sounding like a balloon going down, then he let rip as it roared into a huge raspberry. All the cats except for Sheba had smirks on their faces. They tried to contain their laughter but it was impossible. Sheba tutted and huffed as she jumped off the gold chair, making her way towards the kitchen.

'I've had enough of you all for one day,' she hissed. 'Come on Felix, let's go.'

'Wait for me, Gunner! It's so dark, wait everyone. I'm going as fast as I can,' cried Puss.

'Keep up, Puss, and keep a watch for those amber eyes. They could appear at any time.'

'You're scaring me, Gunner.'

'I'm sorry Puss. We're all nervous about tomorrow.'

'Thank you for seeing me home, Gunner, you're a good cat.'

'Don't worry about tomorrow, Puss, you can do it. Tiger will help you and besides, Rosco may be the meanest cat on Dragon Hill but you're by far, quicker and much more agile at climbing a tree. I've seen you.'

'Really?'

'Now go and get some shut eye. Tomorrow is nearly here.'

CHAPTER 9

Sheba frowned as she watched the heavy rain pound against the window then roll down and gather at the bottom of the glass. This weather wasn't part of the plan. The fast-moving clouds looked angry; the rain had set in for the day. She sighed heavily then looked at herself in the long hall mirror. The hours she had spent grooming her beautiful white fur would all be for nothing.

At eleven o'clock she would have to brave the rain and help Felix and Vinnie collect the netting from the allotments. But it would all be worth it to get rid of Rosco. Then things could get back to normal and Vinnie would disappear back to Church Street. What did Vinnie have planned for Rosco's future? If the plan worked, that was. Would Rosco be sent away in a truck up to the highlands of Scotland? He would have to live with the Scottish wildcats. How would that turn out? Or maybe he would be taken to the zoo where he would spend his days living with wild animals. He was, after all, quite wild.

Felix was also frowning back at his house. He was concerned about his tummy hurting. Why oh why had he been so greedy and eaten so much breakfast, today of all days? He moved over to the window. The rain was starting to ease. He looked at the builder's white van parked outside the doctor's house. Would it ruin their plan? The cats hadn't allowed for an unexpected vehicle to be parked there; it was in the worst possible place. He would talk to Vinnie about it later. But what was Vinnie's plan for Rosco after the capture? Maybe he would be catapulted high into the air, landing on top of the rubbish dump? He smiled as he pictured himself waving goodbye to Rosco as he was blasted up high into the atmosphere in a rocket.

In Church Street, inside the warmth of the hairdressing salon, Vinnie stared at his reflection in one of the many mirrors. He adjusted his collar and checked his teeth. He stood up straight; he was ready for battle. 'Come on my son, let's get over there and get the job done.' He sniggered, as he pictured Rosco trapped inside the camouflaged netting, swinging helplessly from the tree. Ten minutes later he was at the allotments helping Felix and Sheba. They did a practice run to see how fast they could pull up the net.

Vinnie was impressed how all the

cats had worked together. He was most surprised by Sheba this morning though; her white fur was damp and muddy and she hadn't complained once. They loved living on Dragon Hill and weren't going to let any cat or human spoil it for them. It was their home. Vinnie smiled at Felix and Sheba. He had enjoyed being back on Dragon Hill once again, and had missed their company, it had been fun; though he wouldn't be telling them that.

'Righto, let's drag this netting onto the frog and toad. You did a good job Sheba, and so did you, me old tea leaf.'

'I am not a thief, Vinnie; how dare you call me that!' seethed Felix. The three cats worked quickly and efficiently. The camouflaged netting was placed cleverly at the bottom of the road. Vinnie checked the ropes and tucked them out of sight behind the tree; there would be no escape for Rosco.

'I'm a bit concerned by that white van parked outside the doctors house, Vinnie. Will Gunner be able to negotiate around it all right? He'll have Rosco hot on his tail at that point.'

'Went round to his place to warn him, but I couldn't find him anywhere. I expect he's already at your house getting into position Felix. It's nearly time for the off.'

'But what are we going to do with Rosco when we've captured him, Vin?'

'No need to worry your pretty little head about that me old china, I've got it all worked out, you'll see.'

'Well, good luck everyone,' said Sheba, giving her tail a brief last-minute lick.

'Yes, good luck everyone, see you back at the den later,' whispered Felix.

Sheba tutted and shook her head. 'It's the CLUBHOUSE!'

But Felix and Vinnie didn't reply, they had already climbed up into the tree to take their places. Their sharp eyes now firmly fixed on Dragon Hill, concentrating and waiting with anticipation to see a flash of pale ginger stripes come tearing down the hill with the mean grey Rosco in hot pursuit.

CHAPTER 10

There was a deafening drum beat coming from deep inside Puss's chest as she stood at the entrance to her house. A shiver went through her little body as she looked at the cold wet weather. She heard Tiger's voice inside her head. 'This is it Puss. Off you go, stay calm and breathe.' She trotted across the road and over towards the large cherry tree. Leaping up onto the first branch, she climbed up steadily through the wet leaves and soggy branches and sat halfway up clinging to her favourite branch. She didn't have long to wait.

'Oh no, Tiger, I can see him coming. He's on his way!'

Puss sat silently as she stared down from the tree, observing Rosco's gigantic body slinking towards her, getting nearer and nearer. But Rosco paused; he turned abruptly. He was now crouched down, watching and waiting for some poor unsuspecting creature in the bushes. Puss watched on as Dragon Hill's arch enemy devoured a small mouse. The crunching sound coming from Rosco's jaws made Puss shiver; he was indeed a killing machine. This was it! It was time; it was now or never!

Puss scratched at the bark with her claw to gain Rosco's attention. He looked up and saw Puss halfway up the tree looking back down at him. In a split second Rosco leapt at the tree, clambered up at the speed of lightning and hurtled towards her. Puss turned and ran down the other side as fast as she could; she knew this tree well and followed her usual path zig-zagging down through the branches

There was no time to turn to see if Rosco was following but she could hear him getting nearer. Puss was indeed quicker and more agile at getting on and off the tree than Rosco, but the tree was wet and she slipped off the last branch and lost her balance, landing hard onto her back. Leaping up without a moment's thought, Puss skidded then scampered off at break-neck speed. She had never run this fast before in all her life; she had never needed to. Rosco was rapidly catching up, but by now Puss had nearly reached Felix's house. But where was Gunner?

Gunner! Where are you? Why aren't you here? I can't see you; you're supposed to be here! Puss was now panting and starting to struggle. She couldn't keep up the pace for much longer. Tiger's voice pushed her on. 'Come on Puss, you can do it, just a bit further, nearly there.' She ran on past Felix's house with Gunner nowhere to be seen.

Puss now had the doctor's house in view. She could easily swerve in there and escape. NO! She wasn't going to let her friends down. They would be waiting anxiously at the bottom of the hill; she was going to take one for the team.

Puss felt the full weight of Rosco land on top of her, bringing her down to the ground. A searing pain shot through her small body and she meowed loudly as Rosco took a bite out of her ear. The two cats, wrapped tightly around each other, neither one wanting to let go, rolled speedily down Dragon Hill. The wet gravel scratched Puss and cut deep into her skin.

Then something happened; the two cats came to a sudden stop!

They had rolled underneath the builder's van. Rosco's huge furry body was stuck! Puss slid herself out from underneath the van. The neighbours had now come out of their houses to see what all the commotion was about. The people began laughing and pointing at Rosco and he didn't like it one bit. He tried several times to move but it was useless, he was well and truly wedged between the van and the road.

The rain had now stopped and the sun was shining brightly through the clouds as Vinnie, Felix and Sheba left their positions and walked curiously up the road towards the van. 'That wasn't part of the plan, Vinnie?' squeaked a shocked Felix.

'Would you Adam and Eve it?' said Vinnie, shaking his head. 'And where the 'eck is Gunner?'

CHAPTER 11

The three cats trotted over to Puss. Her fur was covered in oil from being trapped underneath the van, and blood was dripping from her tattered ear. Felix patted Puss, smiling at her in admiration.

'I was in serious Barney Rubble, Vinnie, but I didn't give in!'

'I know Puss, you had the opportunity to scarper, but you didn't. Well done me old mate, well done.'

Gunner suddenly appeared, skidding to an abrupt halt in front of the cats.

'Where were you Gunner?' whimpered Puss. 'You didn't show!'

'I'm so very sorry, Puss. I'm so sorry, everyone', he blurted out. 'My owners shut me indoors. They trapped me in the lounge and I couldn't get out!'

'What the 'eck did they do that for then?' demanded Vinnie.

Gunner lowered his head in shame. 'They held me down and squirted me with flea drops on the back of my neck. It was horrible, just horrible. I couldn't move. Look what they've done to my beautiful fur!' he whined, turning around to try and show the other cats.

'Oh, stop complaining,' said Felix. 'Look at poor old Puss, just look at the poor old girl.'

'You should have seen her Gunner,' said Sheba. 'Puss was incredibly brave.'

Gunner swallowed as he looked over at Puss, remembering only too well how frightening it was to have Rosco on your tail getting nearer and nearer, then feeling those

teeth sinking deep into you. He looked a
his shortened tail.

Gunner crouched down and stared a
Rosco still firmly wedged under the var
Rosco let out a large hiss, showing a clum
of Puss's black fur stuck to his broken fang.

The shrill sound of brakes coming to a ha
drew the cats' and neighbours' attention
Nobody recognised the car, an old gree
Land Rover, as it pulled up alongside th
van. The door opened slowly, its hinge
squeaking. All that the cats could see wer
a pair of black muddy boots land on th
ground. The land rover man was small an
round with rosy cheeks and a cheery grin. H
wore a dark green waxy jacket with a brow
tweed cap. One of the neighbours greete
him.

'Oh, hello Farmer Gigglesworth. Wh

brings you to Dragon Hill?'

'Well, I was on my way up to the cat home to find a cat who liked catching mice. You see, I have a terrible mouse problem at the farm, overrun with the little rascals. As it happened, I stopped off at that lovely little bakery on Church street. Their doughnuts are so scrummy,' he replied, patting his tummy and poking the end of his tongue into the corner of his mouth to lick away the last of the raspberry jam. 'Anyway, whilst I was there, I overheard a conversation between two of the customers. They were discussing the problem of a mean and greedy cat who had taken up residency in their street. So, I said to myself, George, this could be the cat for you, and you would be helping these good people of Dragon Hill. Any signs of him today?'

'Oh, he's here alright, take a look under the van,' said the neighbour. 'He's caused trouble here before; you'd be doing us and the cats a big favour if you could take him off our hands. You won't be disappointed either – he is king of the hill at catching mice.'

Farmer Gigglesworth bent down and looked at Rosco trapped under the van. He got the usual unfriendly hiss.

The cats watched on as Farmer Gigglesworth put on his tough leather gloves and carefully pulled Rosco out from underneath the van, placing him swiftly and securely into the cat basket and into the Land Rover. Rosco let out a large hiss and spat at all the cats. His huge paw poking through the wire door of the basket, revealed his long, sharp claws. As the vehicle trundled up Dragon Hill, the cats all cheered with relief. Rosco was gone. Life on Dragon Hill could finally go back to normal.

'Huh?' said Gunner.

'I know, I know, you're all disappointed, aren't you? you wanted Rosco to come to a nasty sticky end,' said Vinnie.

'You bet we did, but what was your plan Vinnie?' asked Gunner.

'Yes, Vin, what was the plan for after we captured him? After all, we couldn't have left him swinging from the tree in that net!' said Felix.

'Oh, I had a plan in mind alright. I thought we should take him to the deserted island not far from here. He wouldn't cause much trouble there.'

'You mean Turkey Island, Vin? The one where nobody lives?'

'Yes Felix, that's what I just said me old

china, if you were listening. I thought that was the best idea, but on second thoughts it would have been a nightmare getting him there, trying to put him in a boat and Sheba complaining that her paws were wet. Nah, I think this was the best outcome alright. And.... he wouldn't dare show his face here again, he's never been so embarrassed, and besides, the farm is miles away. He'll be happy and content being the king of Scratchy Bottom Farm.'

'Everyone to meet back at the old haunt tonight for celebrations, seven pm,' said Vinnie. Sheba gave him one of her looks. 'I mean the clubhouse,' he quickly added.

Gunner could feel tears pinching at the sides of his eyes as he watched Puss slowly limp back up the hill. He followed closely behind.

'I am so sorry I wasn't there, Puss. I feel so

bad.'

'It wasn't your fault, Gunner, please don't feel bad. You were captured and squirted. They got you. It was just bad timing, that's all. Thanks for walking back with me.'

'No worries, see you tonight, Puss.'

Puss winced as she eased herself in through the cat flap of her house. She had never been so pleased to be back home. The warmth from the fire greeted her as she limped into the lounge, plonking herself down onto the rug. She gave herself a light groom. She had done it! She had taken on the mean cat, face to face, and won. There might be a chunk taken out of her ear, and a small bald patch on her shoulder, but it had been worth it. Exhausted, she fell into a deep and contented sleep with dreams of sitting happily in the cherry tree once again.

CHAPTER 12

'Out of my way Felix, you're getting underneath my paws. Go and do something useful,' snapped Sheba.

Vinnie, Sheba, Felix and Gunner had come to the clubhouse early. They were preparing a very special surprise for Puss. Vinnie and Gunner were rolling out a red carpet in the lounge and Sheba was preparing snacks in the kitchen.

'Go away Felix, I've already told you,' she shouted, as she shooed him out of the way. It wasn't going to be easy, keeping him away from the snacks. 'Go and keep watch.'

'Huh, I'm cream-crackered,' announced Vinnie wiping his brow. 'I think we're all done here Gunner.'

'Quick! She's coming!' said Felix, jumping

down from the window. 'Take your places everyone!'

Two minutes later Puss limped into the lounge.

'Surprise!' shouted all the cats, jumping out from their hiding places.

'What's all this then?' stammered Puss, edging onto the red carpet. The cats all looked at her kindly and with gratitude. She was their hero with her torn ear, bald patch and fur splattered with tarmac and gravel.

Vinnie leapt up onto the table. He looked down at the cats. 'Tonight, we have a hero in our midst, let us make no Cadbury's flake about it.'

'Mistake,' whispered Gunner into Puss's torn ear.

'Who's that then? Who's a hero?' asked Puss, looking all around.

'Why, it's you, silly,' laughed Sheba.

'Jump up here, Puss, if you can. We have something for you. But first Sheba is going to say a few words,' said Vinnie.

Sheba joined Vinnie and Puss, then cleared her throat. 'Well, everyone, although our well-thought-out plans didn't go quite the way we intended, and Rosco didn't end up in Vinnie's clutches, we still had a marvellous outcome, and if it hadn't been for you, Puss, Rosco would still be out there now terrorising the neighbourhood, but instead he's...'

'He's terrorising the wildlife down on Scratchy Bottom Farm,' interrupted Felix. Vinnie reached behind him and picked up an orange leather collar, he passed it to Sheba. She stared down at the metal tag. It read Jasbir.

Puss lifted her head up high as Sheba fitted it securely around her neck.

'We have a new name for you, Puss.'

'It's not Peggy is it? I've already got an auntie called Peggy.'

'We hereby name you Jasbir.' All the cats put their paws together and cheered. 'Well done Jasbir, well done.'

Puss looked puzzled. Vinnie explained. 'You are no longer just Puss, you are Jasbir. It means victorious, hero, and triumphant warrior. And the orange collar is for courage. You took on Rosco without any thought for your own safety.'

Puss, or Jasbir, as she was now known, smiled proudly. 'Well, I feel most honoured, thank you everyone,' she added.

'Were you scared, Jasbir, when Rosco was chasing after you?'

'Of course she was, Felix,' tutted Sheba. 'What sort of question is that?'

'I didn't really have time to sit and think about it, Felix. I just got on and did it, although I did have help from Tiger.'

'Let's start on the snacks,' said Felix dashing into the kitchen.

Jasbir went over and sat next to Gunner who had managed to bag the best chair for the very first time.

'What do you think of your new name then?'

'I think I'm getting used to it,' she replied. 'It's a much better name than Puss, more interesting.'

'And what does Tiger think of it?'

'I don't know Gunner; he isn't around anymore. I think he's moved on to someone else who needs a friend, just like I did when

I was Puss. But I have decided that I'd like to be a more interesting cat, a bit like Vinnie in fact. And Gunner, I'm even going to learn some cockney rhyming slang.'

'Trust me Jasbir, you don't want to be like Vinnie.' They both looked over and watched Vinnie dig out a slither of chicken from his teeth, gaze at it then throw it back into his mouth.

'Hey Gunner,' called out Felix from across the room. 'See you've got a nice new collar on today, too.'

'Hmm, I quite like it. My owners managed to get it on me but not without a struggle I might add,' answered Gunner, adjusting it with his paw. 'I think blue suits me, don't you? I wonder what blue stands for? Powerful, suave, handsome? Intelligent maybe?'

'Afraid not, Gunner. It's just the new

range of flea collars from the pet shop in Church Street,' sniggered Felix.

'You're rather quiet tonight, Vinnie. That's not like you,' said Sheba.

'Truth is darling, my plan failed. I failed. All that work you did in getting the netting made and the trap set up,' sighed Vinnie. 'I feel I've let everyone down.'

'Don't take it so personally Vinnie, it all turned out alright in the end, and I'm proud of you.'

Vinnie narrowed his eyes at Sheba. 'Did you just say you're proud of me? You actually said something nice. You 'ave got a cherry tart after all.'

'I'm proud of you because you let Farmer Gigglesworth take Rosco and re-home him and you didn't have to. I know that you really wanted him banished to Turkey Island.'

'Oh no, I'm not turning into a big softy, am I? That won't do, that really won't do at all.'

'And I find myself warming to the new Vinnie. Why don't you stick around? You're part of the gang now,' said Sheba, adjusting Vinnie's collar so that it sat straight.

'Well, I must admit everyone, I am kinda getting used to the old place.'

'Yes, Vinnie, please stick around, we like you,' said Gunner nodding in agreement.

'And besides,' added Jasbir, 'you never know who may return!'

'Rosco wouldn't dare return, the little blighter. He's probably sitting comfortably in the barn, belching at this very moment after gobbling up a large plate of mouseaka. Gunner, you are officially back to being the fastest cat on Dragon Hill. Rosco wouldn't

dare to show his face here again.'
  Would he?

The end

Other books in this series
by Sue Holland

The Russian Princess

Mischievous Mimi

Printed in Great Britain
by Amazon